This book is dedicated to my parents.

www.mascotbooks.com

A Sheep Named Dave

For more information, please contact:
Mascot Kids, an imprint of Amplify Publishing Group
620 Herndon Parkway, Suite 320
Herndon, VA 20170
info@mascotbooks.com

Library of Congress Control Number: 2021923668

CPSIA Code: PRT0622A

ISBN-13: 978-1-63755-148-6

Printed in the United States

A Sheep Named Dave

Lena Schultz

Illustrated by Emily Sullivan

Once upon a time, there was a sheep named Dave who lived on a happy little farm. He spent his days playing with other sheep, lounging in the sun, and cuddling with his mom.

But when Dave was still just a baby lamb, his mom became very sick and couldn't take care of him anymore. Even though Dave loved the farm where he lived, he had to move away to a rescue center where he didn't know anyone at all.

When Dave first arrived at the rescue center, he was still so tiny that he had to sleep in the house with the people who lived there. He was nervous about being in a new place, but the people gave him bottles and took care of him just like his mom had.

And so, day by day, Dave grew bigger and stronger. The people took him to the beach and on hikes, and he became friends with their dog. Eventually, he grew healthy, strong, and big, so he moved outside to live with the other farm animals.

Dave made lots of new friends, but he missed his mom and the old farm and dreamed of finding a forever home with a family of his own.

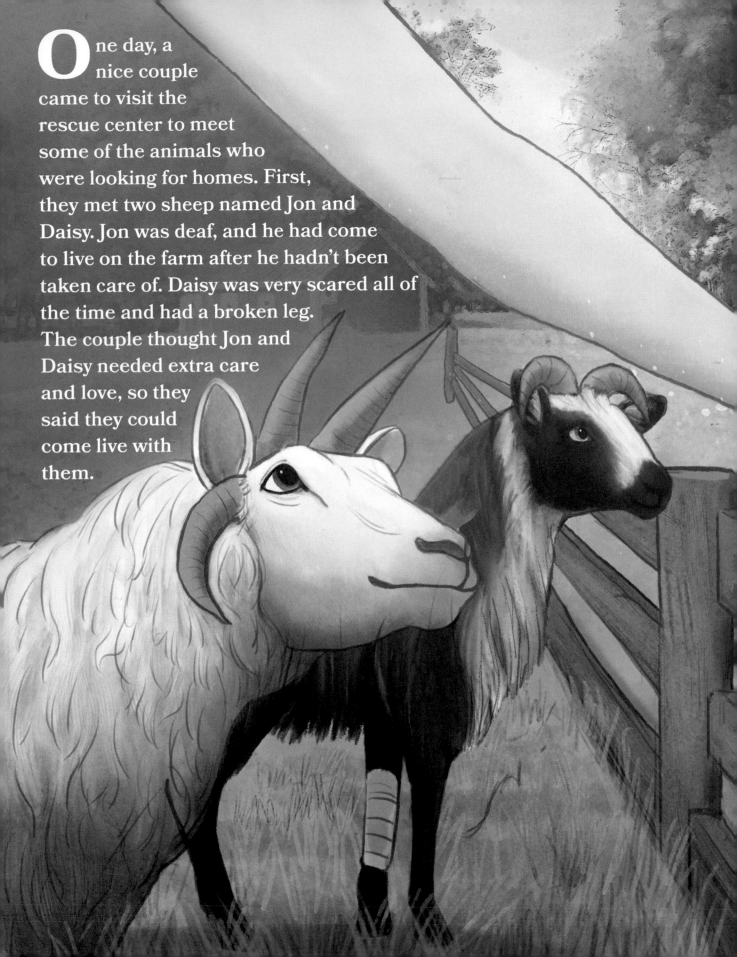

One day, a nice couple came to visit the rescue center to meet some of the animals who were looking for homes. First, they met two sheep named Jon and Daisy. Jon was deaf, and he had come to live on the farm after he hadn't been taken care of. Daisy was very scared all of the time and had a broken leg. The couple thought Jon and Daisy needed extra care and love, so they said they could come live with them.

Just as the couple was getting ready to leave, Dave decided to go over to them too. He was the biggest sheep of all now, and he was still waiting for a home of his own. The couple thought he was so sweet and friendly, and Dave liked them too. He really wanted to go home with them!

The couple soon learned that Dave had been on the farm since he was a baby and decided Dave must be the most special of all. So they adopted all three sheep that day and took them home with them to live on their little farm.

Sometimes change can be hard. When Dave first arrived at his new home with Jon and Daisy, he was scared. But after a few days, he started to feel more comfortable and made friends! First, he met a mama goat and her two boy goats who had been living at the farm for a while already. In fact, the mama goat and her boys were the first animals to move into the farm!

Dave liked the goats, and he liked their names even more. The goats' old owners really loved muffins. They loved muffins so much that the goats were named after certain flavors! The mama goat was called Poppy Seed and her sons were called Banana Walnut and Chocolate Chip. They all had nicknames too, but Dave loved their full names. He wished he had a name like that sometimes.

The goats were a happy little family, but they were excited to share their farm with new friends too. Before long, Dave felt like he had brothers and even a goat mama.

Dave loved his new home and the farm's neighbors. And the neighbors loved Dave. He said hello to them every morning, and they would feed him and take his picture.

When visitors came, Dave was thrilled to meet them too. He would be the first one to greet them, and he made the other animals feel brave enough to do the same thing. The visitors all loved Dave the best. They would pet his thick, white wool, and he would lean against them to say thank you.

Dave even loved to help around the farm. Whenever the barn was being cleaned, he would stand or lie in the middle of it and sometimes taste the new straw being brought in.

Whenever the couple was out in the pastures, he would visit them to see what they were doing and if he could help. And when they were working in the garden, he was a wonderful supervisor and watched everything they planted. He was always excited to see the plants grow.

Even if it was rainy or snowy, Dave didn't care. He loved being outside, and his wool coat always kept him warm.

One day, two new goats came to live at the farm. They were very old and very sad to be there. They loved their old home very much, but the wonderful woman who had them couldn't keep them anymore. She had worked hard to find them a home where they would always be loved and safe.

These two old goats were named Tilly and Zippy, but most often, they were called the Grandma Goats. They were scared at first, just like Dave had been, but he knew what to do.

Dave showed the Grandma Goats where the best places to sleep were, where they could graze on the sweetest grass, and where the creek was for fresh water. He wanted them to feel just as welcome as he had during his first days on the farm.

Pretty soon, Tilly and Zippy felt right at home! Dave made them realize it was a good place to live, and they knew they were safe and loved just like the wonderful woman who brought them here wanted. Dave was so happy they had moved in and was grateful to have two new sisters.

At the little farm, there were also many birds. There were ducks, chickens, roosters, geese, and turkeys, and Dave loved them all. He would sleep next to the ducks every night, and he loved watching the geese swim in their pools. The roosters were loud, and two were so puffy and cuddly that they made Dave smile. He liked how different they looked.

But Dave's favorite birds were the turkeys. Dave liked one turkey named Penguin best of all because he was friendly and made cool noises. Whenever the people went out on their deck or Dave came near him, Penguin would yell, "Gobble, gobble, gobble!" It always made Dave happy. Sometimes Dave and Penguin would take naps near each other in the sunshine on nice days. The couple thought it was really sweet to see how well Dave got along with all the different animals. They were so proud of him.

One day, a big furry dog moved
in. His name was Dude, and he
was a farm dog whose farm was sold, so
he needed a new place to live.
Dude was always happy and never had a bad
day. He loved farm animals and his job of
protecting them. At the rescue, Dave had lived
with a dog, so he was instantly thrilled! Dave
and Dude became friends immediately.

The little farm even had three barn cats who hid a lot during the day but came out at night. They stayed away from Dave mostly, but he thought that was okay. He understood that everyone was different and that those differences made the farm so interesting!

ven with all these wonderful, special animals, the nice couple felt something—or someone—was missing at their farm.
One morning, the couple left and was gone all day. The animals wondered where they had gone, as it was not like them at all to leave for such a long period of time. When the couple finally got home, they gathered all of the animals around. Dave could tell they were excited about something.

The truck opened, and there were two tiny baby cows! They were very small and sick, but the people already loved them. One was spotty and friendly, and his name was Pono, which was a special dog the couple once knew. The other was almost all white with black ears, and the lady thought he looked like a little white deer. His name was Kai, which is Hawaiian for ocean.

They were making sounds Dave had never heard before, but he knew they must be special.

The couple loved these little tiny cows very much, and they had an important job for Dave.

They asked Dave to help the baby cows feel at home, just like he had with all the other animals. They told Dave that the two little boys were just like him—they didn't have a mom!

Dave knew it was important to look after them and was so happy the couple trusted him to take care of them.

That's when Dave realized he had found the family he had always wanted. He had a mama goat and lots of brothers and sisters. He was best friends with a turkey and a dog and lived with two people who loved him very much. And now he was a dad!

The little farm had become one big, happy, and very special family, and Dave couldn't wait to find out who might join next.

Acknowledgments

To my husband, Brian, whose idea it was to buy a farm. If it weren't for him, I wouldn't be on this wonderful journey. Brian, I love you and love sharing this life with you. Living here is the happiest and most rewarding time in my life.

To my parents, Mike and Barbra, who believed in this book from the very first page (and who were my first editors). Mom and Dad, I'm grateful every day for you. Your incredible support and love has made me who I am. I love you, and thank you for all you have done for me and for us.

To my mother-in-law, Diane (and my father-in-law Jim, who is in heaven). Thank you for your support of our life and little farm. I'm so lucky you're my mother-in-law. We get along so well that it often feels like I'm talking with a friend.

To my personal life cheerleaders, Kathy and Michelle. When I told you both that I wrote a book, you were so supportive. You gave me the confidence I needed and never doubted me when I doubted myself. I value your friendships so very much.

To Jamie (and Simon, in heaven), we became friends years ago through my dogs. So much has changed since then, but we have remained close through all of it. Hearing your voice always makes me smile.

To Amy, you are so thoughtful and love our animals and farm so much. Your positivity and bright spirit are wonderful.

Thank you to those who have trusted us with the animals that came to live at Living Aloha Farm:

To Kim and Brian, who brought us Poppy and the boys the weekend we moved in. We began learning right away because of them.

To Betty, who brought the Grandma Goats into our lives. They wouldn't be here without you, and we are so glad for the time with them.

To Anya, who trusted us enough to let the Grandmas stay here. We gained a wonderful friend in you and are so grateful you were with Tilly (and us) at the end and have been able to see Zippy thrive. We love her, and we know she is fully aware she is the favorite goat.

To Sheila, who picked us for Dude. He has been a perfect addition, and we are so happy he is here with us.

To Center Valley and especially Sara. Thank you for all you do for the animals. And above all, thank you for choosing us for Dave. I hope this book shows how much we love him and what a central figure he is on our little farm.

Thank you to Sam and Matt, who chose us for this wonderful farm. You did a great job restoring this cool, old farmhouse. We feel blessed every day.

To Jess, Kristin, and Gillian at Mascot, thank you for guiding me through this incredible process and taking me on. This has been awesome, thank you! To Emily, thank you for saying yes to this project. Your art is amazing, and I love what you added to this book.

Finally, to our other friends and family not previously mentioned. We appreciate all your love and support, in both our little farm and in life overall.

Aloha.

Author Bio

When Lena was a little girl, she would always tell her parents, "When I grow up, I'm going to have whole much doggies." Even at a young age, she knew she wanted to be surrounded by animals every day—and she grew up to do just that.

Living Aloha Farm began when Lena's husband, Brian, found the little old farm for sale in 2019. The two fell in love with the place immediately and decided to open a sanctuary for homeless animals in need of care and love. In 2022, they gained their 501(c)(3) nonprofit status and became an official sanctuary. Today, their animal sanctuary is home to many safe, happy, and well-loved animals, including the ones in this book!

Prior to Living Aloha Farm, Lena and Brian also fostered dogs for local animal rescues and educated against breed specific legislation. They now live with their six dogs and sanctuary farm animals at Living Aloha Farm in Lake Stevens, Washington.